AS IF BY MAGIC

PUBLISHED IN UK NOVEMBER 2020
Republished March 2023

MARKYOURTEXT.COM

THE RIGHT OF MAY PARKER TO BE IDENTIFIED AS AUTHOR
OF THIS WORK IS ASSERTED IN ACCORDANCE WITH THE
COPYRIGHT DESIGNS & PATENTS ACT 1988

THE RIGHT OF SARA FOYLE AS ILLUSTRATOR OF IMAGES
THROUGHOUT THIS WORK IS ASSERTED IN ACCORDANCE WITH THE
COPYRIGHT DESIGNS & PATENTS ACT 1988

THE AUTHOR HAS MADE EVERY EFFORT TO CONTACT COPYRIGHT
HOLDERS FOR PERMISSION AND APOLOGIZES FOR ANY OMISSIONS OR
ERRORS IN THE FORM OF CREDITS

A CIP CATALOGUE RECORD FOR THIS BOOK IS AVAILABLE FROM THE
BRITISH LIBRARY

ISBN: 978-0-9559075-9-3

DEDICATED TO THOSE YEAR 5 EXTENSION READERS
(2019/2020)
I HAD THE PLEASURE TO ACCOMPANY AS WE JOURNEYED THROUGH
EACH WEDNESDAY'S READING EXPERIENCES

YOUR COMMITMENT TO SUCH A HIGH STANDARD
OF READING WAS OBVIOUS
THANK YOU...

A HUGE THANK YOU TO FAMILY AND FRIENDS FOR THEIR PATIENCE IN READING AND GIVING FEEDBACK ON THIS STORY — AND CONSIDERING THEIR AGES SUCH COMMENTS ARE VERY MUCH APPRECIATED!

A *VERY* SPECIAL THANK YOU TO SARA WHOSE AMAZING IMAGES HAVE BROUGHT THIS BOOK TO LIFE — SUCH A CLEVER LADY

EVERYTHING YOU CAN IMAGINE IS REAL...

Sara Foyle 2020

AS IF BY MAGIC

'Who's there?' screamed Pattie. 'Is that you Tom?'

'Shush! It's me, stupid!'

'Don't call me stupid! Argh! Why did I let you talk me into this, and hey, why are you walking so fast? I've tripped twice trying to keep up with you and look, my knees are all muddy!'

'*I* talked *you* into this! *You* insisted on coming and badgered me until I gave in'.

Mumbling to herself Pattie once again brushed the dirt from her trousers and sarcastically whispered, 'Ooh goody, we're going to see badgers; Hmmm!'

'C'mon slowcoach' whispered Tom as he lowered the beam of his torch to check for holes in the path. Falling in front of Pattie would not be a good idea; she'd never let him forget *that*.

*

You might be wondering why Tom and Pattie were out together as daylight was fading, and walking over ground that was uneven and muddy in places. The reason lay with their Year 8 teacher who encouraged her class to 'get out and explore', and six of them decided to do just that. Vic, Brady, Sam and Megan joined with Tom and Pattie to organise an after school meeting to work out a plan.

Excitement within the group was obvious at their meeting, but as Tom quoted the five W's he was about to put to them eyes widened and shoulders rose; they looked baffled. He went on to explain the idea behind the five W's and that in coming to a decision on the first they must move through the other four. The first W was *'who'* should be in charge, and the remainder of the group unanimously voted Tom their captain as he often took charge of team projects in class. Tom immediately named the group 'The Intrepids'.

So, *'what'* would be their challenge? They settled on a search for nocturnal animals; and the *'why'* was simply because these animals are rarely if ever seen by many humans. The question of *'where'* was easy as they all lived near Weston Wood, an area well known for its wildlife such as badgers, foxes, deer, owls and an abundance of bird species. The River Kym meanders through Weston Wood, and near to its south boundary the group found a dilapidated hut which would have been used as a hide by twitchers looking for rare birds. Repairs to the hut started in earnest when a local wood merchant gave the group timber off-cuts which they conveyed to the hut in a wheelbarrow Brady's uncle lent him. Megan *'borrowed'* her dad's hammer and Sam retrieved a bag of nails from his dad's tool shed. Pattie was in charge of snacks and drinks to keep them all going while they worked on restoring the hut.

On the side facing a stream there was a wide, oblong gap in the wood where birdwatchers could see birds taking a dip during the day. The long bench below the gap was no longer safe to sit on so the group set to work with their tools and wood to repair and widen it, and within just a couple of weeks they had themselves quite a comfortable hut, albeit roofless and with only a large hole where a door might once have been.

Happy with the look of their semi-restored hut it was ironically renamed their shelter but in reality, with no roof cover, it offered very little protection from the weather. The final W was *when*? The Intrepids chose the month of May for their first adventure.

Tom and Pattie are friends because they have to be, not because they want to be. They're involved with the school buddy group, set up to look after newbies to help with reading, writing, ICT, maths and friendships, but that's as far as *their* friendship goes.

Writing fictional stories is Tom's favourite hobby and, according to his teacher, he writes to a much higher standard than that expected of a twelve year old. He's the type of student teachers adore as he puts chairs tidily under desks, makes sure books are neatly placed on shelves and likes to organise anything, and anyone, whenever he gets the chance. He's always smartly dressed, solid in stature with thick, black, wavy hair and he's a perfectionist but, when things don't go according to his plan, he can be short tempered and his friends know that's the moment to steer clear.

Pattie on the other hand loves reading factual history, not exploring fictional characters that might change the natural balance of her world. She's a kind-hearted and quite scatty young lady whose strawberry-blonde, curly hair bounces about her shoulders as she walks, and her bubbly character lights up a classroom whenever she enters. She is loved by everyone, well nearly everyone!

*

The weather in late May was warm and dry.

Tom, anxious to get to the other Intrepids and set up quickly, hunker down and watch the action, was rattled because Pattie was late meeting up with him and she kept falling behind.

'At last' whispered Brady. 'We didn't think you were coming, but don't worry we haven't seen any animals yet.'

Tom's look toward Pattie spoke volumes. He put his torch on the bench, its beam highlighting an array of sandwiches, sausage rolls, chocolate bars and paper cups almost overflowing with fizzy lemonade, and zipped open his backpack to retrieve his contribution to the feast.

'Food looks good guys' he said, 'even if there's no action outside there should be plenty of munching going on in here'.

A whisper radiated through the shelter; 'Guess what Tom? I've forgotten my sandwiches and juice!'

Tom was even more rattled. He reminded the group that the Intrepids' rule number two was to enjoy a feast before spending the next half hour or so in silence, listening for those elusive night-time animals and rule number one, he directed at Pattie was to turn up on time with your *own* food and drink!

After they'd eaten, and without the slightest warning, an icy breeze encircled the group, its sharp breath wrapping them as one silenced bundle.

From outside the shelter came a loud, breaking-twig-like noise.

Unwrapping themselves from the invisible icy sheet, the group tipped the now cleared wooden bench onto its side and turned their torches off. They crouched behind the bench showing only a row of knuckles sitting along the edge like birds' feet on a branch. The shelter began to vibrate.

Minutes felt like hours as they waited; for something, or nothing more to happen.

The vibration abated and when it eventually came to a stop, six heads popped up from behind the knuckles. Vic moved to face the others, and turning on his torch he lit up each face in turn whispering, 'so, c'mon Intrepids, who's going outside?'

A whispered chorus of 'not me!' rose into the chilled air.

Cat-like, Tom fearlessly, well almost, crawled to the open entrance and looked out, but he could see only the silhouette of trees against an unusually large full moon.

'Just look outside Tom' whispered Pattie. 'Don't *go* outside or you might get attacked and taken away by a wolf!'

'Thanks Pattie, that's just what I needed to hear right now!' But then...

'It can't be!' exclaimed Tom.

'Can't be what?' demanded Megan. What is it?'

Tom turned to look back at the others saying, 'Well, it looks like candlelight, but who'd be out there with a candle in the wind?'

The other Intrepids quietly exclaimed, 'A *candle!*'

Tom rejoined the others behind the bench as, floating on the now light breeze entering the shelter, the sound of children's voices came closer.

As the brilliance of candlelight filled the doorway the group ducked behind the bench, sucking in air as they did so and holding on tightly. The temptation to look was so strong their heads rose slowly above the bench like six fairground targets waiting for a coconut to be hurled at them, and twelve blinking eyes tried in vain to focus on the apparition. Panic set in and the shelter filled with screams.

The piercing sound subsided and three young children could be seen standing huddled near the doorway, their one small candle now smouldering on the ground. It was difficult to decide which group was the more frightened.

One child, a boy, picked up the candle and held it high. He was about ten years old, his grubby, short grey trousers hanging lopsided on his hips, his vest dusty and feet shoeless. A fine, white dust intertwined with his black, curly and dishevelled hair.

Candlelight fell on his two companions; a boy of about the same age in a similar state of untidiness, and a younger, very pretty girl, her dirty face tearstained, her dark ringlets and plain grey dress streaked with white dust.

The shelter filled with light as each torch was turned on, their beams landing gently on three children still standing by the doorway. Tom walked warily forward.

A Barn Owl's flapping wings caused everyone to look up, and they saw it land on the only wooden beam across the roof space.

Tom's voice broke the silence. 'Who are *you*?' he said directly to the boy holding the candle.

Looking at Tom, the boy in the grey trousers boldly returned his question.

'I'm Tom and these are my friends Vic, Megan, Brady, Pattie and Sam. What's your name?'

'I'm 'arry; this is me sister Mary an our cousin Dani'.

No-one spoke, but as introductions were over the Intrepids righted the bench, replacing what was left of the food and drink, and Harry blew out his candle.

Tom gestured to the visitors to sit down. 'You look tired' he said, 'why don't you sit down? Are you looking for nocturnal animals too?'

Harry chuckled. 'Noct-*tunnel* animals? What are *they*?

'Nocturnal animals' said Tom, 'are animals that sleep during the day and come out to feed at night. That's why we're here; we want to see them because not many people get the chance and, talking of food, why don't you eat with us, we've got some food left?'

Harry's sister, Mary, who was holding on tightly to her brother's arm, released her grip and moved toward the bench. 'I don't think we 'ave those types of aminals where we come from, do we 'arry?' she whispered.

'But surely you must be from around here' suggested Pattie, 'otherwise, how did you get here? And your clothes; they're so thin! You'll freeze to death out here at night.'

'We off'en explore this part of Bidston 'ill after school so we know where we are', replied Harry. 'Somethin' bad 'appened at 'ome an everywhere went black. We got scared an just ran 'till we saw the trees an then we knew we'd be safe 'cos we were on Bidston 'ill.'

'You must have walked a long way', Pattie gently continued, 'because Bidston Hill isn't near here; I've never heard of it.'

The calmness now felt within the shelter was blown away as the owl released a bloodcurdling scream into the night sky.

Mary looked up at her brother and, with her voice broken from a sudden rush of sobbing, she cried 'What's 'appenin' 'Arry? Where are we?'

Harry hugged his sister. 'Don't be scared sis' he said, 'these kids won't 'urt us.'

Megan offered Mary lemonade and a sandwich, but she refused. Harry and Dani said they'd already had their tea. Unease within the shelter was palpable. There were so many unanswered questions.

Tom spoke directly to Harry. 'So, tell us what frightened you at home.'

'Aren't *you* scared?'

'No, why should I be scared?'

'The bombs!'

'*What* bombs?'

Dani interrupted, saying 'Maybe we should stay 'ere 'arry; sounds like we'll be safer 'cos they've 'ad no bombs 'ere.'

'You'd better tell us about the bombs Harry' asked Tom, 'and exactly where you come from.'

Silence fell and all eyes focused on Harry.

'We live in Birken'ed; don't really know 'ow we ended up 'ere.' He sniffed. 'Every night me mam put black material over the inside of all our winders; she said everyone did it. She made us jam butties for tea an then we all sat 'round the wireless listenin' to the man on the news.'

'Do you know what year it is?' asked Tom.

Harry's face beamed, '1941 of course and it's my birthday today, I'm ten!'

Jaws dropped, eyes widened and gasps echoed around the shelter and although his body was trembling, Tom's voice sounded calm as he asked Harry to keep talking.

'The sirens went off when there was an air-raid an then we'd run to the underground station an' 'ide. Mam said we don't 'ave an Anderson shelter 'cause we 'aven't gora garden.'

'What's an Anderson shelter?' asked Vic. 'Is it like this one?'

'No, I don't think so. Mam said they'd 'ave an iron roof an this one's got no roof. She said they're built in the ground too. Everyone's gora gas mask though, an' at school some very small kids gora Mickey Mouse or Donald Duck one. Our Mary's gora Donald Duck one 'avent you Mary?' Mary nodded.

Pattie asked where their masks were.

'They're on our kitchen table' replied Harry. 'We're supposed to carry 'em with us wherever we go, but we forgorrem. Anyway, then the man on the wireless said the docks might be bombed an' me mam was frightened 'cause the docks are only at the bottom of our street. She said we 'ad to go to bed early just in case there was an air raid in the night an we'd 'ave to gerup an go an 'ide. Our Dani lives a few doors away with Aunty Eva an me mam told 'im to go an tell 'is mam we might be bombed. So I got the candle off our table an we went to the front door with our Dani but then a great big wind knocked me over'. Harry flung his arms up and out into the air. 'There was a 'yuge white flash an lots of noise, like a train speedin' through a tunnel. Then we were runnin' on Bidston 'ill. Are you *sure* this isn't Bidston 'ill?'

'I'm sure' answered Tom.

A loud sound outside the open doorway alerted everyone. Might this be an inquisitive animal or more ragged children coming in?

'Who's there?' shouted Vic. No answer came. He shone his torch directly at the open doorway and, although his teeth were tightly clenched, he managed to shout even louder, 'we're not afraid, you can come in.'

All eyes looked to the bottom of the doorway as a large black nose and long red snout slowly edged its way through. Two bright, yellow eyes in a huge head followed the snout.

Pattie let out a muffled scream.

It was a fox; an enormous fox. His whole body was in the shelter now, his bushy red and black tail slowly swishing wide from side to side. He slinked up to where Harry, Mary and Dani were standing. The only sounds were those of short, sharp breaths and the dull thud of huge paws moving across the ground. The fox lowered his head and stretched his thick, strong neck forward. There was no sound but the fox seemed to be whispering to Harry who stood staring at him. After a silent few seconds the fox lifted his head, turned and strolled towards the doorway. He stopped at the doorway, turned back and swished his tail behind him, fixing his eyes steadily on Harry. The Intrepids stood as if frozen in time.

Sara Fowle 2020

The spell was broken when tears streamed down Harry's face as he gently gestured to Mary to hold his hand.

'We've gora go now Tom' he said in a broken voice. 'It was a mistake an we shouldn't be 'ere; we're in the wrong place.'

Dani held Mary's other hand and, with their heads bowed, all three children silently followed the fox into the night.

An icy rush of wind blew through the doorway. The Intrepids fell into a heap on the floor as the shelter shuddered. The owl screeched, spreading its wings to fly into the night sky, leaving behind only a loose feather and the silver glow of the moon to fall onto the human mound. No one moved.

As the realisation of what they had witnessed sunk in, one by one the Intrepids stood, picked up their backpacks and torches and headed home in silence.

Tom went back to the shelter the following day. Crisp packets, paper cups and empty lemonade bottles were strewn over the bench and on the floor. Deep in thought he put all of the waste in a bin-bag he'd brought with him and was about to leave when he saw something white lying beside a large stone near the doorway. Thinking it was more rubbish from the night before he bent to pick it up and found it certainly wasn't rubbish but something amazing.

Would the Intrepids disband? Decisions had to be made. A week after their adventure Vic broke his leg in a skateboarding accident and Megan, Brady and Sam refused to go back to the shelter. The Intrepids were reduced to just two explorers, Tom and Pattie. Tom was rattled.

*

On Monday Pattie caught up to Tom in the school corridor, 'What have you done with the candle you said you found in the shelter on Sunday?' she asked.

'It's in a box at the bottom of my wardrobe.'

'Aren't you scared?'

'Why?'

'Well, because it's... err... sort of weird, isn't it?'

'Don't be daft, it's just a candle.'

'Well, it definitely wasn't in the shelter before those children turned up'.

'That makes it special not weird.'

'I still think it's eerie. Miss Andrews is back tomorrow; should we tell her what happened in the shelter?'

'Not sure, and anyway if we do she'll probably think we made it up. Let's leave telling her anything about the shelter until we've got some info on animals and birds; after all it's hard for us to imagine how we spoke with children from another time *and* saw a huge fox speaking to them. It sounds unbelievable doesn't it? Anyway, c'mon or we'll be late for class.'

The summer holidays passed and Vic recovered from his injury. The Intrepids were now three, and Tom wasn't so rattled.

Heavy rain and storms were forecast for September and October, but that didn't deter the Intrepids who were ready to plan another visit to their shelter.

*

'Aren't teenagers entitled to be more adventurous, more independent and definitely more attractive to the opposite sex?' This was the conversation Tom was having with his mirror image as he reflected on the fine black hair protruding above his upper lip. *'To shave or not to shave; that is the question.'*

Decision made and not a fine black hair to be seen, Tom set off for school. The Intrepids had arranged to meet to organise their next trip; their first this term. Not that term time determined their itinerary, but school holidays did sometimes get in the way of their plans.

'Happy Birthday Tom' roared Pattie across the school yard, 'see you after school, *teenager!*'

Tom raised his hand in acknowledgement, but he was rattled. *'She's so over the top with everything! How can I tell her she drives me nuts?'*

'What's up with the face Tom?' asked Vic as he caught up with him in the classroom.

'Oh, just thinking Vic; don't mind me.'

'Cheer up matey it's your birthday. What presents did you get?'

'Mum bought me an iPhone but I'm not allowed to bring it to school in case I lose it; what's the point of having one if I can't keep it with me?'

'Did you get anything from your dad?'

'No. I haven't seen him since he walked out last month. Mum was annoyed he hadn't even sent a card, but I couldn't care less.'

'You'll be able to take the phone with you when we go to the shelter won't you? It'll be handy just in case we get lost in the dark and need help.'

'I was thinking we'll go during the day this time as it's half term next week; what d'you say, about ten in the morning next Thursday?'

'Sounds good to me matey but what d'you think Pattie'll say?'

'Fete accompli my friend, fete accompli!'

'Okay clever clogs, what does that mean?'

'Decision made, so nothing more to discuss. Here she comes, tagging along with a teacher, probably boring her with all the minute details of her amazing family cruise. Honestly Vic, why does she go on so much about things that don't really matter to anyone else? I'll tell her what we've decided.'

*

Thursday was a calm and sunny day, but because there had been downpours that week the Intrepids decided to don waterproofs and wellies. Their backpacks were bulging with food and Tom brought the candle with him in the vain hope it really did have magical powers. He took the candle from his backpack and held it up in front of him as he walked.

'What *are* you doing?' asked Vic.

'Just giving the candle a chance to create magic *if* that's what it can do.'

'Should it be lit then?'

'I hope not; I haven't brought matches with me!'

'That's stupid!' laughed Pattie, 'how can an ordinary candle be magical. It's just a candle you said, Tom; the one you picked up off the shelter floor.'

'But it was brought there from way back in time wasn't it? So there's no harm in giving it a chance.'

Vic got them off the subject of the candle saying, 'I've got something to celebrate our return to the shelter too, but you'll have to wait to see it'.

For once Pattie was leading the walk but she stopped in her tracks and the boys almost bumped into her.

'What's wrong now?' shouted Tom as he jumped to the side of the path avoiding hitting Pattie's head with the candle by a whisker.

'What if the shelter's flooded?' shrieked Pattie. 'After all, it's by a river.'

'Easy, we'll go back home, but any rain inside the shelter will have soaked through the ground by now and, anyway, we've got our wellies on. Come on, don't be a wimp.'

'*Me*? A *wimp*! How *dare* you Thomas!'

Laughing at his friends' antics Vic walked on and shouted, 'C'mon children, stop arguing and let's see what our shelter has to offer this time.'

As the Intrepids neared the shelter Tom noticed Vic kept smiling, and asked him what he found so funny.

'Oh nothing really; I was just thinking about something which happened last weekend.'

'I worry about you sometimes you know!' Tom said laughing. 'It must've been good if you're still smiling. C'mon spill the beans.'

There was no time for Vic to give an explanation, if indeed he intended to give one, as the group saw something unexpected in the shelter which stopped them in their tracks.

Across the bench lay what looked like a large piece of thick, black material.

Pattie's shriek caused Tom to stick his fingers in his ears. 'Oh for goodness' sake Pattie, it's only cloth.'

'But who put it there? And who put those roses on the bench?'

Tom picked up the cloth and tried to hold it high to see what it was, but it was so long and wide he had to ask Vic to help him. Although the bottom of the cloth lay in concertina folds on the floor it was obvious from the shape which was now emerging between Tom and Vic that this was a cloak, a large cloak, and one worn by a very large person. They lay the cloak back on the bench.

The red roses lacked thorns and looked freshly cut, but this was Weston Wood and roses like that didn't grow in woods. Pattie picked them up.

'Oh they're beautiful' she said, 'and they smell lovely, but without water they'll shrivel and die. I've got a bottle of water; have either of you got a cup or something to put this water in?'

Vic was standing at that part of the bench nearest the doorway and was opening up his backpack when he felt an arm encircle his arms and chest and lift him high into the air. He let out a frightening scream.

Tom and Pattie stretched their necks in order for their eyes to view the enraged face of a man squashing Vic's body to his huge chest with one arm, the other wielding a hunting knife across his throat.

Vic's natural dark skin colour turned pallid and his large brown eyes bulged. 'Please don't kill me' he choked.

The intruder spoke and his voice was as big as he was. 'Stop your squirming boy or I'll slit your throat right now! And you, little lady, they're *my* roses, put them down *right NOW!'*

'B-b-but I was going to put them in w-w-water so they don't d-d-die' stuttered Pattie. 'P-p-please don't hurt my f-f-friend.'

'Why are *you* here? Did not the Lord of the manor send you to kill me?'

'Lord of the manor?' queried Tom as calmly as he could muster, 'who's he? And why would he want you dead?'

The intruder's grip on Vic tightened, his frown deepened and the knife moved closer to Vic's skin.

'Because I picked a few of his *precious* roses for my daughter, Bella,' he grunted. 'But I persuaded him to release me so I might give my other two daughters the gifts he willingly gave to me. I put those gifts into a large travel chest. Did you not see my carriage and horses in the wood?'

'No', came Tom's stifled answer, 'and we're definitely not here to kill you.'

Tom's adrenalin pumped violently through his veins; his heart raced and his mind ran through dozens of scenarios trying to find a way to save his friend. For what felt like far too long he was speechless, but a flash of inspiration struck and suddenly he knew what to do. With his vast knowledge of the meanings and morals behind folklore and fairy tales he remembered the tale of Beauty and the Beast. He took a chance on this mystical apparition being the merchant who, in the story, gathered roses from the Beast's private grounds and avoided death only by saying he'd give up one of his daughters to the beast.

Pattie was still holding the roses.

Tom moved gingerly towards her and whispered, 'Pattie! Remember Beauty and the Beast? Act like the merchant's daughter who asked him to bring her a rose! Quick! *Now!*'

Pattie's eyes grew wide and her throat dried up but, seeing Vic's life in the balance she conjured up enough mental control to walk towards the intruder and sweetly say directly to him, 'You're such a kind and honourable man and I know you don't want to hurt my friend. I believe you picked these roses for Bella because that's all she wished for, and they're beautiful with their intense perfume and deep red colour'. Pattie held the roses momentarily to her nose before holding them high. 'Take them; I was admiring them and trying to find a way to keep them fresh for you. *Please* don't hurt our friend' she cried.

At that moment Vic's body became limp, his head fell forward and his hands hung lifelessly at his sides. The intruder felt this change and very cautiously laid Vic's small unconscious body on the bench.

'I do not wish to hurt you' he said, his voice more gentle now. 'But I *am* afraid you might prevent me getting home. I gave my word to the Lord of the Manor I would return to him within three months. He would have killed me in his garden as I cut away those roses, but having raised his sword to strike he held back and said it was Bella he wanted, and that I should give her up to him. I knew then I could persuade him to give me more time. Bella would willingly give up her life for me, but I will not allow her to do so. Although I am ready to die for her I do not intend to breathe my last breath here.'

Looking directly at Pattie he said, 'you, my dear child, look so like my beautiful Bella and you are brave to challenge me. I will not harm such a beauty nor indeed your dear friends. Give me the roses and I will take my leave.'

Pattie, having already placed the roses onto the bench and picked up her bottle of water was leaning over Vic, gently splashing drops of water onto his face. He murmured and slowly opened his eyes.

'There you are' whispered Pattie, 'we thought we'd lost you, but Tom's idea worked and we're safe now.'

Opening his sandwich box Tom directed a suggestion to the merchant. 'There's no reason for you to go right now; would you like something to eat before you leave?'

'I'm obliged to you but I must be on my way. There is a deadline to meet and I must make haste' replied the merchant as he swung his cape up and around his wide shoulders creating a gust of wind which blew Pattie's hair about her face. He picked up the roses and made his way to the doorway, but before reaching the opening he turned, and taking one rose from the bouquet he gave it to Pattie, bowing as he did so.

'Farewell my new friends' he said, 'maybe we will meet again one day.'

As Pattie watched the merchant leave the shelter tears welled in her eyes and she held the rose tightly to her heart.

'If I wasn't holding this rose' she cried, 'I would never have believed what just happened!'

Vic, having regained his strength said to Tom, 'the first thing you did when you came into the shelter was to put *that* candle on the bench; so do you think it really does have magic powers and it brought the merchant to the shelter?'

'No! Obviously he had already been here and left his cloak and the roses before going back outside for some reason. Unless...' Tom hesitated, 'maybe because I took the candle out of my backpack before we got here it's magical energy got to work and *that's* when the merchant was brought here; but how can we know for sure?'

The group forgot they were at the shelter to look for various species of birds and instead set out their lunch in silence, each pondering what they had just witnessed. Was the shelter itself a supernatural space, or *was* it the candle left by the children from 1941 which held the magic?

Pattie broke the silence saying that she will preserve the rose by pressing it within a page of one of her books.

'D'you have a copy of Beauty and the Beast?' asked Tom.

'I never thought of that; yes I do' said a smiling Pattie, 'and thinking of that *fairy* tale, how can a fictional character from someone's imagination appear in our shelter? That's impossible. Isn't it?'

'Did you know' said Tom, 'the story of Beauty and the Beast was first published in 1740?'

'What!' exclaimed Pattie, 'that long ago?'

'Yes' replied Tom with pride at his knowledge. '*And*, stories

like Jack and the Beanstalk may have grown from tales told about four or even five thousand years ago!'

'Gosh Tom you're so clever.'

'Not really; I just like reading about myths, legends and folklore and that's where fairy tales come from you know. And, you'll love this Pattie; the very first fairy tale was written by a French *woman* back in 1690 when she published her story and called it a fairy tale.'

'Cor!' exclaimed Vic, 'that's cool Tom; I never knew that.'

Pattie was so excited she blurted out, 'you're *amazing* Tom and, to think you're my very *best* friend.'

Tom was rattled.

'What I'm trying to say' Tom continued, 'is that fairy stories come from tales told thousands of years ago, and many stories had some truth in them because they included *real* people.'

'So' said Pattie excitedly, 'you mean we actually saw a real-*live* ghost – *again*!?'

Tom and Vic were laughing loudly, and emphasizing every word they said 'Yes, a *real, live, ghost!*

Tom added '*as if by magic!*'

Controlling his laughter Vic said, 'you must admit though Tom, Pattie was brave wasn't she?'

'Well, I *suppose* she was, but don't forget Vic, if it hadn't been for my brilliant idea you'd be dead now!'

All tensions disappeared and the group's laughter grew even louder.

'Is that rain?' suggested Vic.

'Hey?' Questioned Tom, 'then how come it's raining but we're not getting wet?' He looked up expecting to see sky and feel rain, but all he could see was a grey metal corrugated roof. 'Who put that on?' he exclaimed.

Vic couldn't hold back his delight. 'My dad did! He came here last weekend and put it on for us, and on our way here I was wondering how long it would take you to notice; that's why I kept smiling.'

'Three cheers for Vic's dad' exclaimed Pattie.

Pattie continued to hold on to the rose whilst she ate her lunch, and each of the Intrepids relayed their feelings about what they had experienced. What, they wondered, might be the next magical scene to play out in their now fully roofed shelter, and will there be another mysterious keepsake to take home with them.

One decision made without hesitation was that when they next visit the shelter they must take with them both the candle and the red rose which by then would be pressed and dried within Pattie's book. The other decision was that they would return in December, especially now there was a roof on their shelter to keep them dry.

*

Snow was not forecast for Christmas so the Intrepids decided their last visit to the shelter this year would be during the day of 24th December.

The weather was predicted to be unseasonably warm and, as sunset would be around 4.30pm, they chose to be at their shelter by lunchtime armed with plenty of mince pies, hopeful that this time they might experience an apparition with a Christmas theme.

In addition to UK birds such as Robins, Blackbirds, Blue tits, Long-tailed tits and Goldfinches often seen in family gardens, the Intrepids planned to search out the little Nuthatch, a bird which can walk head first down a tree trunk as it has specially adapted feet to help it cling to the rough surface.

Tom was particularly excited to be visiting the shelter again as his mum gave him permission to take his iPhone with him, and so he was able to promise his teacher he would take photos of any birds the Intrepids were able to see from their shelter.

'You look a bit peaky Tom; are you feeling okay?' asked Vic.

'I think I'm getting a cold, or something, but I'll be alright. I'm looking forward to this trip too much to be sick.'

Pattie gently touched Tom's arm, 'I've been worried about you Tom. Where've you been; I've not seen you for weeks?'

'I don't really want to talk about it right now.'

'Okay' said Vic, 'as long as you're okay we don't need to know any more. So c'mon matey let's get going, it's nearly lunchtime and there's a magical shelter waiting for us.'

The three Intrepids, wearing sturdy boots and warm, waterproof coats just in case the predicted mist and fog came down earlier than expected, started on their final expedition of the year.

There was much more light than earlier in the year as most of the trees had shed their leaves, but evergreens continued to stand majestically along one side of the vast wood.

'Don't you think the wood feels different today somehow?' asked Pattie.

Tom said nothing, but Vic commented that he felt sadness all around him.

'Yes, I feel that too' said Pattie. 'Should we turn back?'

'*No!*' demanded Tom. 'We *must* go on and complete today's trip; it's important.'

'What's so important about today?' asked Vic. 'Do you know something we don't know?'

'I've really got to make this trip; that's all you need to know.'

'That's weird' said Pattie. 'What's so special about you?'

'Nothing' said Tom, 'nothing at all.'

*

The final part of the walk to the shelter was taken in silence and as they got nearer the group grew more anxious with each step. Every few minutes Vic and Pattie's eyes met with one of those *"what d'you reckons is happening"* looks.

Tom's pace quickened. 'What time is it?' he asked.

'Time you got yourself a watch' laughed Pattie.

'*Not* funny!' exclaimed Vic.

'Oh! *Sorry*. I thought a bit of humour would lighten the mood; silly me!'

Without turning to look back at Pattie Tom asked her if she'd brought the rose with her.

'Yes of course, I said I would. Have you got the candle?'

Tom looked forlorn as he took the candle from his coat pocket and turned to face Vic.

'Here Vic' he said in a hushed whisper, 'why don't you keep it now? Where I'm going I don't need a candle.'

'What's that supposed to mean?' exclaimed Pattie.

'You'll see. Trust me.'

Vic took the candle from Tom. 'I don't like the sound of that Tom, but if you want me to have it I'll keep it safe.'

They walked on in silence.

Light mist, falling from the now darkened sky gently surrounded the group and Pattie shivered. 'I don't like this' she whispered, her warm breath shifting the mist about her face. 'I definitely, definitely think we should go back.'

'We might as well keep going' said Vic, 'we're nearly there.'

They were only yards away from the shelter when there was a loud rumbling sound and the earth beneath their feet shuddered.

The three Intrepids instinctively threw themselves to the ground as they saw their shelter explode. Pieces of wood and corrugated roof were sent flying through the air as orange flames vomited from what was left of the shelter.

The Intrepids lay still and silent for what seemed an eternity; the silence was deafening.

*

'Tom! Wake up. *Please* wake up' pleaded Pattie.

Tom didn't move.

Pattie held one of Tom's hands and Vic the other and they squeezed ever so gently to try to encourage him to wake up.

Tom's eyelids flickered and very slowly he opened his eyes.

'Where am I?' he asked without looking at anyone in particular.

Vic responded, 'You're in hospital matey. Can you see me?'

Tom took his gaze away from the ceiling and looked around the room he found himself in. He saw Vic on one side of the bed and Pattie on the other, and his mum and dad were standing at the foot of the bed crying, holding on to each other as if at any moment one of them would fall.

'What are you doing here dad? I thought you'd left us.'

Laughing through his tears Tom's dad said, 'As if you'd get rid of me that easy Son! No, I've been away on business and came straight home when your mum rang and told me you were in hospital.'

Tom looked across to his mum. 'Is that true?'

'Of course Tom' she said. 'Don't you remember?'

Pattie was wiping away tears from her cheeks when Tom looked over to her.

'Why are you crying?' he asked. 'And you Vic, what are you doing here?'

'We're here because we love you and we've been really worried about you matey' said Vic. 'You've been in a coma for weeks and your mum asked us if we wanted to come back and see you today because it looked as though you were coming out of it.'

'Really!' exclaimed Tom. 'You didn't get hurt then? What about the shelter? Is there anything left of it?'

'What shelter?'

'The shelter in the woods the three of us have been going to for months.'

'We haven't been near the woods and I don't know anything about a shelter. I think you've been dreaming matey.'

'What's the date Vic?'

'It's Christmas Eve.'

'But we were on our way to the shelter today when it exploded. Is that why I'm here; because I got hurt?'

'No Tom, you've been in here for weeks.'

Tom looked to Pattie. 'Have you still got the rose the merchant gave you?'

'I don't know what you're talking about' said Pattie, 'but look! I've brought you the rose you gave me for my birthday; I pressed it in one of my books.'

'Which book?'

'Beauty and the Beast; you're the beast and I'm the beauty of course!' she said with a laugh.

'So,' said Tom, 'we haven't got a shelter in the woods and we didn't see children from 1941 there, or the merchant who stole roses from the beast's garden?'

Vic and Pattie were shocked and Pattie exclaimed, 'why would we go traipsing through the woods Tom? And we've definitely *not* seen any ghosts!'

Conversations ceased as the door opened and a nurse entered the room followed by a man who looked suspiciously like the merchant Tom remembered from the shelter, but this time wearing a white hospital coat. The doctor officiously told Tom's visitors to leave the room.

The nurse introduced Tom to Doctor Marchant and explained he was going to make sure Tom had recovered from his illness.

Tom asked the doctor why he was in hospital and was told he had contracted a virus a month ago which caused him to collapse and become very unwell to the point he had to be given oxygen by intubation.

'It was touch and go,' the doctor explained, 'but thankfully you're a strong young man, you've beaten the virus and you're back on the ward. All we have to do now is build up your strength before you go home.'

As the nurse was taking Tom's vital signs she said, 'You're a very lucky young man Tom; keep making progress like this and you'll be out of here by New Year.'

'But that means I'll miss Christmas' yelled Tom.

'Oh no you won't, we make sure our patients enjoy Christmas even though they're in hospital.'

For Tom the exercise of making sure he had come through the virus and coma sufficiently seemed to take ages but, when the nurse had completed her assessment and the doctor was satisfied with those results, they were about to leave the room when the nurse picked something up from a chair by the door. She turned back to Tom.

'Oh, I nearly forgot, another friend of yours left this at reception for you; looks like a Christmas present!'

When he was alone Tom unwrapped his mysterious present. He gasped; his eyes filled with tears and emotion shook his body. He was once again holding the spent candle.

Vic and Pattie might not have been to the shelter in the wood but Tom knew he had definitely been there, and he firmly believed that what he could remember happening *must* have happened. This unexpected Christmas present was all the proof he needed.

Composing himself, Tom smiled and read aloud the message on the present tag...

For our friend Tom from Harry Mary and Dani
With our love forever xxx

I hope you enjoyed reading this short story which I wrote during the main Government lockdown of 2020. I realised just how much I was missing working with my weekly groups of 9 and 10 year old extension readers at a junior school near to where I live, and this has been my way of re-establishing a quasi contact and to express my thanks to them for their commitment and friendship.

The apparition of the merchant and his roses evolved in my imagination from the fairy tale 'Beauty and the Beast' (La Belle et la Bête) written by Jeanne-Marie LePrince de Beaumont and published in 1740. Beaumont was a French teacher, journalist and author of many classic tales for children and her tale of Beauty and the Beast stems from real-life events dating back to the 1500's.

The moral emerging from the tale of Beauty and the Beast identifies the need for us all to value inward characteristics, for instance kindness, over only superficial features such as wit and appearance. That moral is recognized when Beauty acknowledges Beast's inward qualities and falls in love with him regardless of his unattractive outward appearance.

The first apparition in the story where young children, lost, frightened and supernaturally fleeing terror, brings to mind the harrowing moment in time suffered by families living in Birkenhead and Liverpool during the 'May Blitz' of 1941. Although Birkenhead docks was the main target for air raids, 11,000 homes in streets radiating out from the Dock Road were completely destroyed and more than 3,000 people killed in those raids.

The philosophy of war is complex and continues to be the subject of debate within our world.

I think there is a need to include release and support for the reader when relaying potentially upsetting facts within a tale, which is why the magical fox and owl came into the story as friendly and helpful guides for those children lost in time.

I'm hoping a sense of kindness, love and friendship comes to light within this story as well as taking its reader on a mystical journey with friends.

I was born in Birkenhead in 1947 in a house on a street near to the docks, and there were gaps within the terraced houses where some had been bombed in the raids of May 1941.

When I was a teenager I enjoyed the 'Mersey Sounds' of the 1950's and 1960's. I worked for many years in a legal office in Liverpool and travelled from Birkenhead to Liverpool over the River Mersey on the MV Overchurch ferry boat which was later re-named MV Royal Daffodil.

In 2008 I wrote a comic book for my grandson for his ninth birthday and he drew the images which were excellent. I have also written many short stories and articles for magazines. I live in Cambridgeshire with my husband, son and Golden Retriever 'H' but, unfortunately for me, my daughter and two amazing grandchildren who are now in their twenties live in America, and of course I miss not having them near me.

Printed in Great Britain
by Amazon

19605418R00037